SO YOU WANT TO BUILD A LIBRARY

by Lindsay Leslie   illustrated by Aviel Basil

CAPSTONE EDITIONS
a capstone imprint

Published by Capstone Editions, an imprint of Capstone
1710 Roe Crest Drive
North Mankato, Minnesota 56003
capstonepub.com

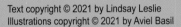

Library of Congress Cataloging-in-Publication Data
Names: Leslie, Lindsay, author. | Basil, Aviel, illustrator.
Title: So you want to build a library / by Lindsay Leslie ; illustrated by Aviel Basil.
Description: North Mankato, Minnesota : Capstone Editions, [2021] |
Audience: Ages 4-7. | Audience: Grades K-1. | Summary: The reader is put
in charge of building a fantastical library where everything is possible
including a waterslide, zip line, really large ladders, and of course, a
full-service sudae bar.
Identifiers: LCCN 2021002332 (print) | LCCN 2021002333 (ebook) | ISBN
9781684463763 (hardcover) | ISBN 9781684463732 (pdf) | ISBN
9781684463756 (kindle edition)
Subjects: CYAC: Libraries--Fiction. | Books and reading--Fiction.
Classification: LCC PZ7.1.L473 So 2021 (print) | LCC PZ7.1.L473 (ebook) |
DDC [E]--dc23
LC record available at https://lccn.loc.gov/2021002332
LC ebook record available at https://lccn.loc.gov/2021002333

Designed by Kay Fraser

Printed in the United States   4624

To Knox,
who would love to have a hot tub in his library. —L.L.

To my family, Amarel, Dani, and Ella. —A.B.

You love books.
You love the worlds in books.

You love the characters who live in the worlds in books.

And you believe there is no better place on Earth than where stacks and stacks of books are kept—the LIBRARY! So you want to build your own.

The BEST. The BIGGEST.
The most MIRACULOUS library ever!

You start from scratch. First, a location. But where?

Here?

There?

OH, YES! Right. Here.

With all this space, it's going to take LOADS of building materials, so you grab whatever you can find.

A little of this.

A lot of that.

A WHOLE LOT MORE OF THAT!

In order to build a library, you need help.
LOTS of help. Thank goodness for friends . . .

. . . and giants.

Time to get to work! You build OUT, OUT, OUT . . .

. . . and UP, UP, UP. Way up!

With windows perfect for daydreaming.

So, what do you want to put in your library?

BOOKS, OF COURSE! ALL KINDS OF BOOKS!

Books about
princesses,
cowpokes,
princesses who are cowpokes,
intergalactic soccer stars,
pie-baking snails,
cartwheeling giraffes,
roller-skating sloths,
and guitar-strumming emus.

Books for HER. Books for HIM. Books for THEM. Books for everyone and anyone—even giants!

A PLAYGROUND? Why not!

The BIGGEST, CUSHIEST, FLOOFIEST CHAIR
you can find? Sure!

A BATHTUB? No question about it!
Reading in the bathtub is your favorite.

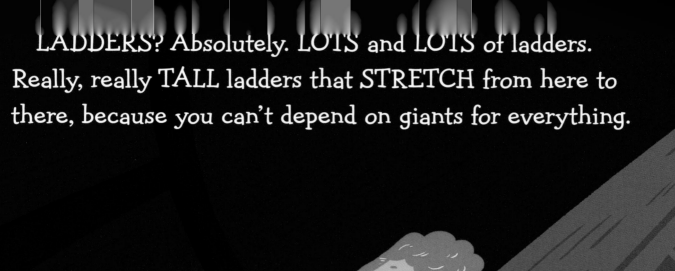

LADDERS? Absolutely. LOTS and LOTS of ladders. Really, really TALL ladders that STRETCH from here to there, because you can't depend on giants for everything.

DRAGONS? Definitely. Every book—and library—is made better by dragons. Make sure the dragons are trained though.

And don't forget about TEENY TINY NOOKS
for teeny tiny fairies with their teeny tiny books.

Then there's the WATERSLIDE,
the wall-to-wall TRAMPOLINES,
the ZIP LINE from the top floor all the way
to the bottom, and the CONVEYOR BELT
from the bottom floor all the way back to the top.

And NO library would be complete without . . .

. . . a full-service SUNDAE BAR!

You get as many scoops as you want since you built this place.

Now that you're full—and so is your library—you probably need to rest. Building a library is hard work.

That can only mean one thing: IT'S STORY TIME!

You grab a book from the shelves.
You cozy up with a snuggle.
Which book do you pick?

So You Want to Build a Library?

PERFECT CHOICE.